TV MONSTER

TV MONSTER

Rosalind Barden

Crown Publishers, Inc.

New York

In memory of Mama

Published by Crown Publishers, Inc., 225 Park Avenue South, New York, New York
10003 and represented in Canada by the Canadian MANDA Group
CROWN is a trademark of Crown Publishers, Inc.
Manufactured in the United States of America.
Library of Congress Cataloging-in-Publication Data
Barden, Rosalind. TV monster/Rosalind Barden.
   Summary: A young boy turns into a TV monster after watching too much
television and is mistaken for Colonel Bop by aliens who take him aboard their
flying saucer and whisk him into outer space.
   [1. Television—Fiction. 2. Science fiction.] I. Title.
PZ7.B250057Taav 1988   [E]—dc19   88-358
ISBN 0-517-56934-5

10 9 8 7 6 5 4 3 2 1

First Edition

One day I won a TV set.

I turned it on and kept it on.

I watched it so much...

I turned into a TV monster.

My dog wanted to play,

but I didn't even see him.

"Behold!" cried General Gop. "Here is my brother —
Colonel Bop—lost on an expedition long ago! And
he has found a TV! We will go home and celebrate!"

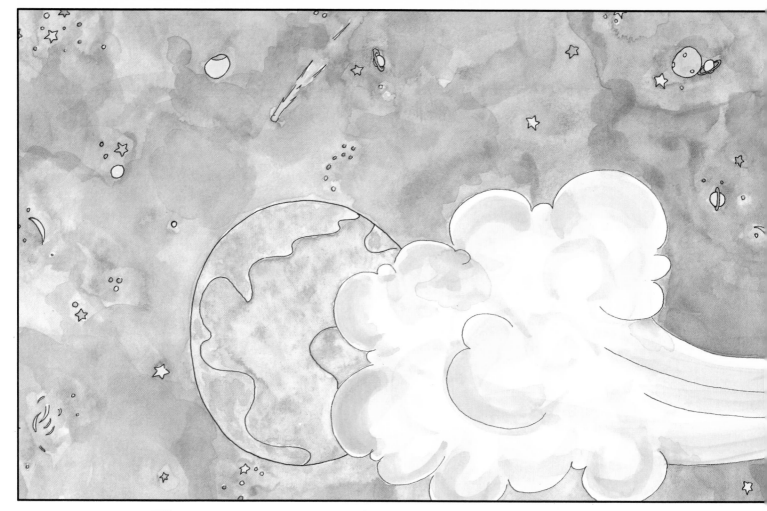

The monsters, my dog, my TV, and I blasted off
into space.

My TV's picture was getting fuzzy, but I watched
it anyway.

We landed beside a gigantic TV set.

"Ever since Big TV broke," announced Gop, "we have been without a set. But now, Bop has given us LITTLE TV!"

The monsters carried me away from my TV.
"Hip Hip Hurrah!" they shouted and tossed me into
the air. I dropped with a thud.

"What's happening?" I said. I had turned back
into myself.

"This is not Bop!" snarled Gop. "And he's got our TV!" said the others.

The whole planet was after us.

My dog found a used-ship lot.

I picked the fastest, fanciest machine.

Luckily, my dog could fly it.

He steered by the TV—the stronger the picture,
the closer we were getting to Earth.

Finally, Earth was in sight.

But my dog had stared at the TV too long! He
was one of them!

General Gop was almost upon us, and I had to
save my dog.

I threw them my TV.

Happy with the set, the monsters flew away.

We were home...

my dog and I,

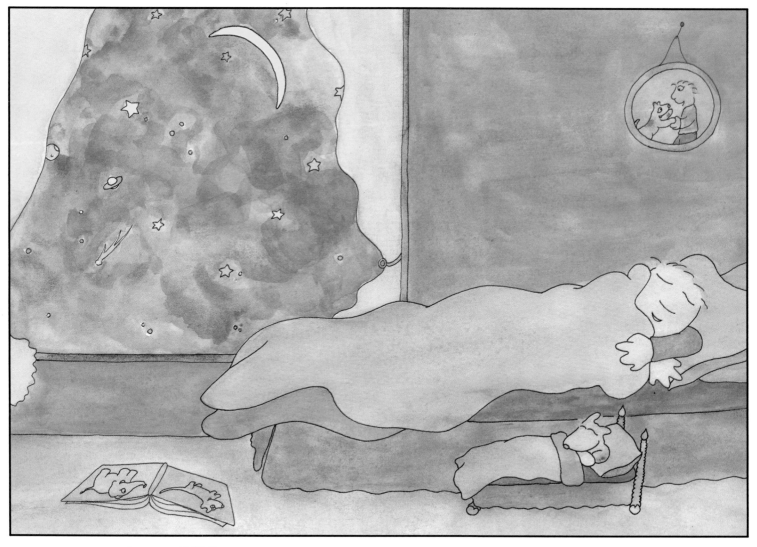

and no TV.